For Shannon, at whose hooves I lay the blame for all of this
—D. H.

To Jean Webb, for all of your love and support
—M. S.

First published in the United States of America in June 2011 by Bloomsbury Books for Young Readers
www.bloomsburykids.com

For information about permission to reproduce selections from this book, write to
Permissions, Bloomsbury BFYR, 175 Fifth Avenue, New York, New York 10010

Library of Congress Cataloging-in-Publication Data
Hale, Dean.
Scapegoat : the story of a goat named Oat and a chewed-up coat /
by Dean Hale ; illustrated by Michael Slack. — 1st U.S. ed.
p.   cm.
Summary: Each time something goes wrong in the Choat household Jimmy blames the pet goat, Patsy Petunia Oat,
who tries to tell the truth about Jimmy's misdeeds but neither Mr. nor Mrs. Choat can understand her language.
ISBN 978-1-59990-468-9 (hardcover) • ISBN 978-1-59990-469-6 (reinforced)
[1. Blame—Fiction. 2. Behavior—Fiction. 3. Goats—Fiction. 4. Humorous stories.] I. Slack, Michael H., ill. II. Title.
PZ7.H129675Sc 2011   [E]—dc22   2010035698

Art created in Photoshop, using digital painting and collage techniques
Typeset in P22 Rakugaki
Book design by Donna Mark

Printed in China by Toppan Leefung Printing, Ltd., Dongguan, Guangdong
2 4 6 8 10 9 7 5 3 1 (hardcover)
2 4 6 8 10 9 7 5 3 1 (reinforced)

All papers used by Bloomsbury Publishing, Inc., are natural, recyclable products made from wood grown in
well-managed forests. The manufacturing processes conform to the environmental regulations of the country of origin.

SCAPEGOAT

The Story of a Goat Named Oat and a Chewed-Up Coat

DEAN HALE

illustrated by

MICHAEL SLACK

I'm stinky.

BLOOMSBURY

NEW YORK BERLIN LONDON SYDNEY

ON MONDAY, when Jimmy Choat came home with no coat, his mother asked him, "Where is your coat, Jimmy Choat?"

The family's spare goat,
Patsy Petunia Oat, raised
her head, coughed, and said,
"He left it in the park."

But Mrs. Choat did not speak the language of goats and listened to her son Jimmy instead, who said, "My coat? It was eaten by P. Petunia Oat."

ON TUESDAY, Pa Choat wanted to watch *The Love Boat* and asked Jimmy Choat, "Where is the TV remote?"

The pet goat, Patsy P. Oat, raised her head and said, "Jimmy threw it away."

But Papa Choat, like Mama Choat, could not speak Goat and listened to his son Jimmy instead, who said, "The remote? It was eaten by Patsy the goat."

ON WEDNESDAY, Mama found her keys in a muck moat and wearily croaked, "Who blew their nose in my tote?"

The Choat goat, Patsy P. Oat, raised her head and said, "Jim did. It was nasty."

But, as you know, the mother Choat did not speak Goat, so listened to her son Jimmy instead, who said, "You know that goat, Mrs. Oat? She sneezed in your tote."

ON THURSDAY,
Jimmy was sick, all day
passing gas from a bad
piece of bass that he
ate the night past.
    The goat was outside,
chewing the grass with
some sass.

ON FRIDAY, Baby Choat's boat would not stay afloat, and Mama asked Jim, "Did you break Baby's blue boat?"

The Choat goat, Patsy P. Oat, raised her head and said, "He hit it with a rock."

But still Mrs. Choat did not understand the goat, so listened to her boy Jimmy instead, who said, "Not me, Mama Choat. I saw the goat break the boat."

ON SATURDAY, the Choats' next-door neighbor Bert Sproat found the goat Patsy Oat with a poorly shaved throat.

So Mr. Sproat presented the goat to the Choats. "Might this be your goat?" asked the good citizen Sproat.

"Why, yes!" said Mr. Choat. "And she has a shaved throat!"

He called Jimmy and asked, "Did you shave our goat's throat?"

The bare-throated goat bobbed her head, shivered, and said, "He did. With *your* razor."

By now we all know Mr. Choat could not speak Goat, and of course listened to Jimmy instead, who said, "Nope. That silly old goat must have shaved her own throat."

But the neighbor Bert Sproat knew the language of Goat,
and heard the whole anecdote of Patsy P. Oat.

Long story short, Dad got the report;
they held family court and gave Jimmy
an old pile of socks to re-sort.
    Patsy looked on with a smirk and
a snort.

But Mr. Bert Sproat well knew the nature of goats and told Patsy outside, "You should not gloat, Mrs. Oat. I know what really happened to Jimmy Choat's coat."